American Frontier #12

DAVY CROCKETT MEETS DEATH HUG

A Historical Novel

By Ron Fontes and Justine Korman
Illustrations by Charlie Shaw
Cover illustration by Dave Henderson

DISNEP
PRESS

NEW YORK

Look for these other books in the
American Frontier series:

Davy Crockett and the King of the River

Davy Crockett and the Creek Indians

Davy Crockett and the Pirates at Cave-in Rock

Davy Crockett at the Alamo

Johnny Appleseed and the Planting of the West

Davy Crockett and the Highwaymen

Sacajawea and the Journey to the Pacific

Calamity Jane at Fort Sanders

Annie Oakley in the Wild West Extravaganza!

Wild Bill Hickok and the Rebel Raiders

Tecumseh: One Nation for His People

FIRST EDITION
1 3 5 7 9 10 8 6 4 2

Library of Congress Catalog Card Number: 93-71032
ISBN: 1-56282-495-3/1-56282-496-1 (lib. bdg.)

Consultant: Michael Robertson, Park Ranger, Program Services
David Crockett State Park
Lawrenceburg, Tennessee

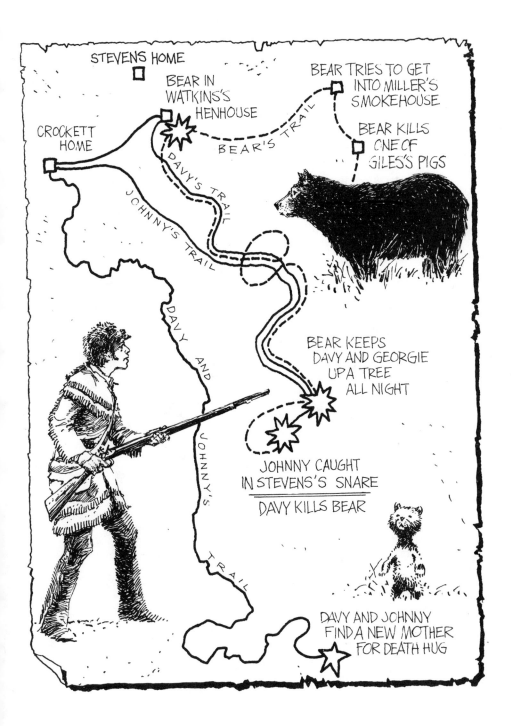

CHAPTER 1

"Gator!" shouted Georgie Russel from the bank of the swamp.

Davy Crockett spun around in the shallow swamp water. "He's got to be twelve feet at least!" Davy called back. He tossed his rifle to Georgie and slipped the hunting knife from his belt. The alligator swam toward Davy, who dropped into a crouch.

"Come on!" Davy told the alligator. Suddenly there was an explosion of white water as the alligator lunged.

Davy and the alligator rolled over and over until Davy didn't know which end was up. He finally managed to drag himself to his knees, his knife clenched between his teeth. He had to admit that this was one of the most ornery critters he'd ever tangled with.

Georgie hoisted his rifle to his shoulder. "Stand clear!" he yelled, cursing as the alligator whipped Davy back and forth. He could not get a clear shot.

Suddenly Davy caught the alligator under its front legs, immobilizing it just long enough to use his hunting knife. Davy let out a triumphant whoop. He was grinning from ear to ear.

Exhausted but happy, Davy stood up and brushed the wet hair out of his eyes.

"Sorry, Davy," said Georgie, tossing him a soggy, scraggly coonskin cap. "I thought it was more important for me to stay here and keep your rifle dry." Georgie smiled and added, "If you'd stood clear, I might've shot that critter."

"Shucks, Georgie," said Davy. "Me and that gator was just having us a little dance, that's all."

Davy wiped his knife clean on his damp buckskins before tucking it back into his belt. He wrung the water from his dripping fur hat. "At least we've got something for the boys to eat tonight."

Georgie made a face. "You intend to eat that monster?" he asked.

"Reckon I do," said Davy. "Gator meat tastes just like chicken."

Georgie gave his friend a skeptical frown. "If you like your chicken long, scaly, and mean as the devil!"

"Now, Georgie," Davy said calmly, "there's no call to carry on. I know you don't like gators." He grinned. "Though they do seem *awfully* fond of you!" The two men laughed heartily, then Davy said more seriously,

"Anyway, we've all been hungry too long to be picky."

"You're right as rain," said Georgie. "We ain't seen nothing else on this huntin' trip, and I wasn't keen on returning empty-handed to a camp full of hungry soldiers."

"Well, we're all feeling a bit ornery on account of this Creek Indian war dragging on," Davy said.

"The truth is, Davy," said Georgie wearily, "I'd rather face a hundred angry alligators than one more of them Red Stick braves." He shook his head. "Don't they know Chief Red Eagle already surrendered?"

Davy paused thoughtfully. "The Creeks are mighty angry," he said after a time. "They trusted the white man's promises that they wouldn't push the Creeks off their land. But the white settlers kept coming. Chief Red Eagle and his Red Stick warriors gave up trusting us." Davy turned to Georgie, who was scratching his head fretfully. "Look at it this way. If someone tried to force you off your land, wouldn't you fight back?"

"You're darned right I would!" Georgie said.

"Well, the way I see it," Davy said, "the Creeks are doing the same thing. Maybe it ain't the best way exactly, but I don't know that they have much of a choice."

"Maybe you're right," Georgie conceded. "But I'll sure be glad when all this runnin' around rounding up renegade Creeks is over and done with!"

Davy agreed. It had been a long year.

The previous August, Chief Red Eagle had led his Creek braves in an attack on Fort Mims in Alabama. In retaliation the United States declared war on the Creeks. Davy and Georgie had been hired by General Andrew Jackson to supply food to his troop of Tennessee Volunteers. A year later, in 1814, Chief Red Eagle surrendered at the Battle of Horseshoe Bend in Alabama. Jackson pardoned Chief Red Eagle, but the Creeks were forced to give up huge chunks of their land. Many of the Creek braves refused to give up. These renegades retreated into Georgia and Florida. General Jackson and his troops had gone after them, and Davy and Georgie had agreed to stay on.

It had not been an easy campaign. The weather had been miserable and the fighting intense. They were always short of supplies, and there wasn't a man—Jackson included—who had had a full meal in weeks. Even so, Davy figured the Creek braves hiding out in the woods had it worse. At least Davy had a *home* to go home to.

Georgie was still in the mood for grumbling. "Why don't we just leave them Red Stick braves alone instead of chasing them all over creation?" he muttered. "I've got so danged many mosquito bites I feel like one of Polly's pincushions!"

Davy laughed, but at the mention of his wife he suddenly grew homesick. "It would be awful nice to get out of these buckskins once and for all," he said.

"Amen to that!" Georgie agreed.

"We'd better head back to camp before it gets too dark to see," Davy said. "Tramping through the woods at night is one thing, the swamp's another."

Georgie agreed. "All this damp muck already looks alike to me." He slapped at a mosquito. "Dang!"

"Gimme a hand with this gator," Davy said. "Take ahold of that tail. I'll take the snappin' end."

Georgie cringed as he gingerly grasped the alligator's tail. They heaved it up onto their shoulders.

As they sloshed back to camp through the mucky water and the heat, their soaked buckskins pulled at their tired legs, and with each painful step the alligator grew more and more heavy. Their faces streamed with sweat.

Davy's wet buckskins steamed in the heat and humidity. The sun only peeked through the dense canopy of trees, but the heat pressed on them like a hot, damp towel.

"If this is spring," griped Georgie, "I'd hate to see summer."

Davy wiped his forehead. The sleeve of his buckskin shirt stank of mildew and swamp. "We'd better be home by summer, or Polly will kill me," Davy said.

Georgie laughed. "Why, I swear you fear that

pretty little woman more than Ol' Hickory Jackson or all the Red Sticks put together."

Davy chuckled. "I'd put Polly and her frying pan against an army any day!"

Finally, they spotted smoke from a fire in the army camp.

"Halt! Who goes there?" demanded a sentry. His blue uniform was streaked with swamp muck and sweat.

"Just us, you idjit," Georgie snapped.

"Brought some supper, Lem," Davy said.

The soldier grinned when he recognized Davy. "I've got more good news!" he said. "We're going home! Got the orders while you were gone."

"Hallelujah!" Georgie whooped.

Davy could hardly believe his ears. Though he often joked about Polly's fearsome temper, he missed her terribly. And he missed Johnny, Billy, and little Margaret, too. That he could finally go back to his farm in Tennessee filled Davy's heart with joy.

That night Davy sat contentedly before the crackling campfire. Overhead the stars shimmered in the sky.

A huge kettle of gator stew simmered over a fire. It wasn't much of a feast, but all the soldiers were glad to have something solid to eat for a change. This had been a hungry campaign from start to finish. Many times, short of food, General Jackson's army had been forced to forage for whatever they could find, including nuts. To-night, though, the mood was festive.

"It does taste sort of like chicken," Georgie conceded. "Still," he said, grinning, "I keep expecting it to bite back."

"What're you going to do when you get home?" Lem asked.

Georgie sighed. "Gonna sleep for a month, and when I wake up I'm gonna eat hot biscuits, fried chicken—and I mean real chicken—and black-eyed peas swimming in gravy. What about you, Davy?"

Davy wiped his greasy fingers on his buckskins. "I just can't wait to see my family! You know, I been thinking, and I calculate Johnny's about old enough for his first rifle. He did all right when we went hunting bears last winter. Reckon my army pay will get him one fine Kentucky rifle."

Georgie yawned. "What I reckon is that the sooner we get to sleep, the sooner we get to go marchin' out of here! I can't wait to get out of the swamp and into a town where I can buy me a bath!"

Two weeks later the weary troops arrived in Winchester, Tennessee. They were home! True to his promise, the first thing Georgie did was buy a bath. Davy, meanwhile, spent his time locating a gunsmith.

"Figured I'd find you here," Georgie told Davy as

he joined his friend in the shop. "The barber said this was the finest gunsmith in town."

"I've got it narrowed down to these three," Davy said. He showed his friend three new Kentucky rifles, just the right length for a boy of Johnny's height.

"There are targets right out back," the gunsmith said. He handed Davy a box of lead balls and a horn of powder.

"Thank you kindly," Davy said.

Behind the gunsmith's workshop was a row of wooden posts. Each post had a large nail driven into the top. One after another, Davy loaded each rifle, carefully sighted down the barrel, and matter-of-factly shot the heads off the three nails.

The gunsmith gasped. "You hit the nail on the head every time."

Georgie chuckled. "No wonder. Don't you realize who you're talkin' to? This here is Davy Crockett!"

"Don't go on now, Georgie," Davy protested. "These are all mighty fine rifles," he told the gunsmith. "But I reckon this middle one is the best."

The gunsmith stared wide-eyed at the man in the coonskin cap and filthy buckskins. "Davy Crockett. *The* Davy Crockett?"

"Reckon one's enough," Davy said modestly.

The gunsmith slapped his hands together. "Why, I'll be proud to know your son is using one of my rifles," he gushed. He pumped Davy's hand. "In fact, I'll give you a possibles pouch and powder horn for free. It'll be worth it to be able to say, 'Davy Crockett bought a gun here.' "

"That's mighty kind of you," Davy said gratefully. A possibles pouch was a small leather bag that was slung over the shoulder. In it a man carried just about anything and everything he could *possibly* need. Davy reached into his own well-worn possibles pouch, pulled out the gold "cartwheels" that were his army pay, and settled up the bill.

"See, I told you," Georgie said outside in the street. "It's worth tooting your own horn now and again."

"Now, Georgie, you know I don't hold with bragging," Davy said. "It's only proper before a fight."

Georgie grinned. "Well, you may not like bragging, but you can't stop me! Mr. Crockett, don't you think it's about time you got yourself home?"

Davy slapped his friend on the back. "Lead the way, Georgie!"

CHAPTER 2

Georgie's voice was hoarse by the time he and Davy had covered the ten miles to the backwoods settlement of Bean Creek, Tennessee. On a hill just beyond Bean Creek, the Crockett cabin was nestled deep in the woods.

Davy thought his homesickness would ease as he got closer to home, but with his approach his ache grew.

By the time he and Georgie rode up the path that led to the cabin, Davy was so anxious he could barely stay in the saddle.

Two towheaded boys ran down the path to greet their father. Davy was astonished. Johnny and Billy had shot up like weeds since he had last seen them in early winter. Davy jumped from his horse and gathered up the two boys in a hug.

"Did you chase down the last of those Red Sticks?" Johnny asked excitedly.

"Did you bring us any presents?" Billy wanted to know.

Davy's throat choked with emotion as the boys ran on ahead toward the cabin. He had hewn the logs himself—and built the stone chimney, too, which he noticed was just a little bit crooked. To the east could be seen the gentle blue rise of the Cumberland Plateau.

Polly stood on the porch, looking pretty as a picture in a pink calico dress. Her brown hair was twisted in neat braids around her face.

"Oh, Davy!" she cried as she came running. "I'm so glad you're home!" Davy flung his arms around Polly. He had thought of this moment so many times in the last year. He hugged her tight. "It's good to be back, Polly," he whispered to her tenderly.

Whirlwind, Davy's oldest hunting dog, cantered around his feet and yipped. Davy grinned. "Whirlwind! Still chasing your own tail?"

Georgie laughed. "That's all he ever chases. And you said he'd outgrow it."

Davy shrugged. "Whirlwind just loves hunting so much. Rabbits and coons aren't always around, but his tail's always ready to give him a chase. 'Course, might be my fault for naming him Whirlwind."

Little Maggie wobbled up and tugged at Davy's buckskins. Davy lifted her up and gave her a big kiss.

"Are you boys all finished with your war?" Polly asked.

Davy nodded. "Reckon I've seen enough fighting to last a lifetime. How about you, Georgie?"

"Amen to that!" Georgie declared.

"Well, come on inside then," Polly said, throwing open the heavy plank door. "I'll have supper directly."

Davy stepped slowly over the threshold, savoring the moment. The cabin was just as he remembered it. Moss and clay stuffed the chinks between the logs, and Polly's cooking pots hung over the stone fireplace at one end of the room. At the other end was the big bed, heaped high with homemade quilts. Davy had thought of that warm bed often while struggling to fall asleep on a soggy bedroll in the Florida swamps.

A ladder led up to the rafters and the loft where Johnny and Billy slept. The furniture included a few trunks and the table and chairs that Davy had hewn from logs. To some folks the Crockett cabin might not seem like much, but to Davy it was a palace.

Polly chattered as she stirred an iron pot suspended on a swinging hook over the fire. "So much has been happening around here, I don't know where to begin. The Millers up the creek have a new baby boy. And the Pottses' daughter finally got married. Can you imagine?"

Davy shrugged, knowing Polly didn't really need an answer. Her face was pink with heat from the fire. The soup she stirred was starting to smell good. Davy's stomach growled impatiently.

As she stirred, Polly glanced over her shoulder. "The Watkinses are having a terrible time, though," she went on. "Most of their cows took sick, and Etta May wore herself to a frazzle trying to make up for the loss by churning butter to sell and by taking in wash. Now she's got an awful fever."

"That's too bad," Davy said. But he couldn't keep the smile off his face. He was so glad to hear Polly's voice, even carrying bad news.

"Some new folks called Stevens have settled over on that hill above the Watkins place," Polly said.

Davy stretched out his legs and brought his feet closer to the fire and sighed. "It's starting to get crowded," he said.

Polly wagged her spoon at Davy. "Now don't you even think about moving again!" she scolded. "And, are you planning to stay put for a while, Mr. Crockett, or will you be running off on a hunting trip or some other foolishness that will keep you away from home?"

Davy hesitated. "Well, a hunting trip ain't exactly foolish. . . ."

Polly set her hands on her hips. "How dare you even think of such a thing!" she fumed. "Why, I've got enough chores piled up to keep you busy till next Christmas!"

Davy got to his feet and put his hand on Polly's shoulder. "Don't you worry none, Polly," he said. Davy smiled and gave her an affectionate squeeze.

"Now," he declared, turning to the children, "how could I forget? I've got presents for each of you. And a very special one for Johnny."

Davy unfurled his blanket roll and presented Maggie with a store-bought rag doll. Billy got a penny whistle, which he put to immediate earsplitting use.

Next, Davy handed Johnny the flintlock rifle.

"For me?" Johnny asked, his eyes as wide as saucers.

Davy chuckled. "Well, I already have one, and this one's a mite short for me."

Billy stopped blowing his whistle and eyed the rifle jealously.

"Now, don't you worry, Billy," Davy said. "You'll get one as soon as you're old enough."

"Can I hold it?" Billy asked. He struggled to raise the rifle to his shoulder. "BAM! BAM!" he shouted.

Georgie shot his hands up. "Please don't shoot," he said, playing along. "I'll turn over all my valuables."

"You will?" asked Billy, surprised.

To the children's delight, Georgie produced three sacks of penny candy. He gave Polly a bar of perfumed soap.

"Thank you, Mr. Russel," Polly said. She sniffed

at the fragrant soap. "It's heavenly. But you needn't have bought me a gift."

"Just trying to assure my welcome," Georgie said.

Polly smiled. "You know you're always welcome here," she said.

"I almost forgot," Davy said teasingly. He pulled one more present from his blanket roll. It was one of the most beautiful bonnets Polly had ever seen.

"Landsakes, Davy! You spent all your army pay on presents," Polly said. "Times are hard. You know the fall crops weren't much, and that was the roughest winter we've spent in a while."

"We'll get by," Davy assured her. "We always do."

"Pa," Johnny said, "with this rifle, you and me can bag that rogue bear. Plenty of meat on her!"

Polly tried to shush Johnny with a look, but it was too late.

"Rogue bear?" Davy asked. "Why didn't you tell me, Polly?"

Polly put her hands on her hips and frowned. "Because I didn't want you running off chasing some dangerous animal before you've had some home cooking and a proper bath and spent some time with your young'uns!" she declared.

"This big old bear has been killing livestock and scaring farmers," Johnny rattled on. "Everybody's talking about her. They say she can't be killed, Pa! She's as big as a tornado and twice as mean. But I bet we could bag her."

"First you'll have to learn to shoot," Davy said. "And I'll have to rest a spell, too."

Johnny's shoulders slumped in disappointment. "Aw, Pa!" Johnny sighed.

"He's right," Polly told Johnny. "Now wash up for supper, all of you."

After several heaping helpings of Polly's home cooking, Davy and Georgie put their feet up before the fire.

"Reckon the missus wouldn't mind if you camped here for a few days," Davy said, casting a hopeful glance at Polly.

"Of course Mr. Russel will stay," Polly said. "I wouldn't hear of him traveling when you're both so exhausted."

Georgie smiled. "I can't argue with that, or with your cooking, Mrs. Crockett."

"Then it's settled," Polly said. "I'm sure the boys won't mind sharing the loft with their uncle Georgie."

"They're bound to be better company than the mosquitoes and snakes down in Florida," Georgie said. "Not to mention the soldiers!"

Everyone laughed.

CHAPTER 3

"Shucks! I missed!" Johnny cried, and stamped a foot in frustration. The echo of his last shot still rumbled and rolled through the green hills. Johnny was having his first shooting lesson.

"At least you stayed on your feet," Georgie pointed out.

Johnny blushed. His first shot had had such a powerful recoil that Johnny had been knocked backward and right off his feet.

Billy had broken out into a fit of hysterical laughter, and Davy had wisely sent him back to the cabin to help Polly with the laundry. The fact is, it was all Davy could do to keep from grinning himself. To his credit, however, Johnny had dusted himself off and quickly tried again.

"Don't worry now, Son. Shooting isn't as easy as it

looks," Davy said. "It takes time to learn, and a powerful lot of patience."

"Not to mention bullets," complained Georgie good-naturedly as he poured more molten lead into the bullet mold.

"Now take your time and measure out just a pinch of powder," Davy instructed.

Davy smiled as he watched Johnny fumble awkwardly with the powder. Johnny spilled as much down the side of the barrel as he got into it. Then he rammed a small deerskin patch and a round lead bullet down the barrel, too. He lifted the gun to his shoulder and squinted his eyes down the shiny metal shaft.

Johnny was concentrating on the log target across the field when his father quickly pulled up the barrel of the rifle. "Hold on there, Johnny," he said. "Someone's coming."

Five men wandered from the woods into the clearing and picked their way across rows of fresh green corn shoots.

"We heard the shooting and figured you must be home!" Dan Miller called out, and waved. He was a burly man with a bushy beard and a ready laugh. He carried a jug. "Is that Johnny shooting up all creation?" he asked.

"Sorry to hear that Etta May took sick," Davy told Tom Watkins, who was standing next to Miller.

Watkins nodded his thanks.

"Welcome back!" said John Potts, tipping his broad-brimmed hat. Potts was out of breath from the walk.

"Help yourself to some spring water," Davy said. Potts mumbled, "Much obliged," and gratefully stuck the dipper into a bucket by the well.

Behind Miller was Davy's old friend Elmer Giles. Giles hadn't a speck of hair on his head but was blessed with the most luxurious white beard Davy could recall seeing. Behind Giles was a man Davy did not recognize.

"Like you to meet our new neighbor," Giles said by way of introduction. "Esau Stevens."

"How do," Davy said. Stevens was tall and thin and wore a tall-crowned black hat in a style popular in the cities. Instead of the moccasins Davy and his friends favored, he wore heavy knee-high leather boots.

"So you're the famous Davy Crockett?" Stevens said. "You're all I've been hearing about since I moved to these parts."

Davy shrugged modestly. "Folks do like to flap their jaws."

"Esau moved here a few months ago from out around Tyler," said Giles.

Davy whistled low. "Is that a fact?" he said. Stevens nodded. "That's a mighty long way," Davy said. "What brings you so far from home?"

Stevens puffed up his chest. "Well, Tyler was getting a little too crowded for my tastes, so I decided to try my hand at frontier life. I figured I'd do a little hunting, trapping, fishing. The fact is," he concluded boastfully, "frontier life is in my blood."

Georgie looked skeptically at Stevens. "You ever do any hunting before?" he asked.

Stevens turned and looked sharply at Georgie. "Not exactly," he conceded. "But I read a lot about it before I came out here."

"What exactly did you do back in Tyler?" Davy asked.

"I ran a dry goods store," Stevens said proudly.

"Well," Davy said, "I don't know much about running a dry goods store, but I do know something about hunting and trapping. If you need any help—"

"Thanks all the same," Stevens said sharply, "but I don't need no help."

Davy shrugged. "Suit yourself," he said. Then Davy laid a friendly hand on Georgie's shoulder. "Mr. Stevens, this here is my best friend, Georgie Russel."

Reluctantly Georgie extended a hand to Stevens. "Pleased to meet you," he grumbled as they shook hands. Georgie had formed an instant dislike for Davy's new neighbor and didn't feel any need to hide that fact.

"You'd be wise to learn a few things from Davy here," Georgie suggested to Stevens.

Stevens grinned humorlessly. "I suppose you're a

famous hunter, too," he said. "You never miss a target, grin the coons down from the trees, spit bullets, and all that."

"I'm not half the hunter Davy is," Georgie replied icily, "but I hit my mark when it counts."

"Well, you must be good," Stevens snickered, "if you can shoot anything with them Kentucky rifles." He shook his head. "Me, I use only the best. The Pennsylvania rifle is the finest there is." Stevens held out the rifle he carried with him.

"Mighty fine looking rifle," Davy said, admiring its elegant silver inlaid barrel and polished stock.

Stevens smiled. "Like I said, nothing but the best."

" 'Course, it's not the gun but the man behind it," Georgie said. "And there's nobody in Tennessee or the whole wide world who can shoot better than Davy Crockett."

"That's what we're counting on!" Giles said. "Reckon you and Davy can help us all out of a jam."

"You know we'll try," Davy said.

"It's like this," Giles said. "Old John here has lost some cows to a she-bear."

"That's right unusual," Davy said. "But Johnny told me there was a rogue bear roaming these parts. What do you reckon would make a bear leave the woods like that?"

Watkins looked sharply at Stevens. "Esau was hunting her," he said coldly.

"Well, she got into my smokehouse," he said defensively.

"It was a hard winter," Watkins said, "and food was mighty scarce."

Davy nodded. "Reckon she woke up mighty hungry after that hard winter. The aroma of a smokehouse full of meat would be hard for any bear to resist."

"That darned bear went straight for the ham I'd been saving for Easter!" Stevens complained.

Georgie chuckled. "Bears don't give a hoot for holidays or proper invitations," he said.

Stevens was not the sort of man who took kindly to interruptions. He glared at Georgie. Then he cleared his throat. "I didn't have my gun with me," he said, turning toward Davy, "so when I heard the ruckus, I took a torch and beat her away. I singed her fur pretty bad, too.

"Well," he went on, "after I drove her away, I got to thinking she'd be coming back. So I got my gun and tracked her. She had just run down the hill right onto the Watkins place. I took a shot at her. But I tell you the bear won't be killed!"

"That's because your shot hit her cub," Watkins grumbled.

"That'll rile up a she-bear like nothin' else!" Davy said.

"Had cubs, did she?" Georgie asked.

"Just the one," Stevens said.

"How can you be sure?" Davy asked.

"I know what I know," said Stevens crossly.

"You think you know everything," Watkins muttered. "Why, I'm surprised you don't try to teach the cats how to chase mice."

Stevens's long face turned bright red. "Well, anyway," Giles said mildly, "since then, that critter has gotten a taste for livestock. Killed one of my pigs just the other day."

Miller nodded and said, "She tried to get into my smokehouse, and she killed my best dog. That bear's got to be stopped."

"A bunch of us have raised money for a reward," Giles said.

"A reward?" repeated Georgie, suddenly intrigued.

Davy stroked his chin thoughtfully. He knew Polly would be mad as thunder. "Usually the meat, hide, and oil are enough reward," he pondered aloud. "But I sure could use a bounty!"

Georgie broke into a huge grin. "When do we leave?"

CHAPTER 4

Polly pulled the last clothespin off the line and tossed the clean laundry into a cane basket. There'd be no time for it to dry today, not with a storm clearly coming.

Polly lifted the basket and walked over to join Davy and Georgie, who had returned from Johnny's shooting lesson.

"What did the neighbors want?" Polly asked.

Davy stared off a trifle guiltily into the distance. "Oh, it was just a sociable call," he answered casually.

Polly looked at Davy, then at Georgie. Her eyes darkened with suspicion.

"They said there's a reward for that rogue bear!" Johnny blurted out excitedly.

Polly threw down the basket and glared.

Davy took a couple of steps backward and smiled innocently. "Now don't get all flutterated," he said, trying to calm her down. "They *also* said that this she-bear hasn't been seen for a while. For all we know," he said in a carefree tone, "she may have left these parts. Bears usually avoid folks, anyway."

"I hope she's gone for good!" said Polly, glowering. Davy and Georgie looked sheepishly at one another.

"Don't you want Pa to get that reward?" Johnny asked.

Polly shook her head emphatically. "I want your father to stay home," Polly said. Davy sighed but said nothing. Polly turned to Johnny. "And I want you and Billy to go over to the Watkins place. I've made up a basket of food to give to Etta May. You may stay and play with Tommy for a little while. He's probably been lonesome, with his ma sick and all. Just try to get back before the rain starts."

Johnny was about to object, but his father caught him with a do-as-your-ma-tells-you look. Johnny reluctantly put away his rifle and fetched the basket.

Georgie grinned. "Reckon I could use one of those food baskets myself," he said brightly. He lifted off his broad-brimmed hat and scratched his head. "My stomach's growling like a spring bear."

For the time being Polly appeared relieved—Davy, too. "You sure it's a bear?" joked Davy. "I calculate your condition might have something to do with that gator you ate. Seems like he's been snapping inside you ever since."

"Reckon so?" Georgie affected a worried expression.

"Well, we better feed him," Davy said, "or there's no telling what'll happen."

Polly smiled. "Come along then, you two. I'll have supper on directly."

Davy and Georgie obediently followed Polly back into the cabin.

"Do you really think that bear has left the area?" Georgie asked around a mouthful of crumbly corn bread.

Davy shrugged. "There's no telling what a bear will do."

"That Esau feller killed her cub," Georgie said. "If you ask me, bears are plenty smart enough to hold a grudge."

Davy agreed. "I heard once about a man who tried to steal a cub. The mama bear followed him for three days. When she caught him, she chewed his leg sore. He got loose and ran off again. She kept following him and eating him piece by piece till there wasn't nothing left of him."

Polly shuddered. "Oh, Davy! Must you tell such stories?"

"It's all as true as preachin'," Davy said, putting his hand over his heart. "I calculate this bear is out for revenge, too."

"Think we can catch her?" Georgie asked.

"Reckon that's hard to say," Davy said. "No two bears are alike. Some are always on the move, some stay put in one place all their lives." Davy gave Polly a quick sidelong glance. " 'Course, it wouldn't hurt for us to do a little looking next time we're out hunting."

Polly frowned and slapped Davy's hand away from the cooking pot.

Georgie grinned. "Reckon not."

Georgie stretched out his legs and tipped his broad-brimmed hat over his eyes. "Wake me when your pretty wife is ready to put food on the table," he told Davy.

Johnny was telling Tommy Watkins about his new rifle when dark clouds began to spread over the sky and thunder began to grumble in the distance. Mr. Watkins, hoeing weeds in his corn patch, hoped to get one more row done before the storm. A bony old horse cropped grass in the yard, and a few spotted cows wandered aimlessly in a field.

Johnny looked up at the sky. "Billy and me better go before this rain starts or Ma will tan our hides," he said.

Just then Tommy noticed his dog, Fang, hunched low and slinking toward the henhouse. Fang stopped at the henhouse door, bared his fangs, and suddenly began barking.

"What's Fang all riled up about?" asked Johnny.

"Let's go see!" Tommy said. "It sounds like it's over by the chicken coop."

"Maybe there's a fox!" Billy said excitedly.

From inside the henhouse the boys could hear the chickens squawking and flapping up a storm. Fang bared his teeth and growled and clawed at the henhouse door.

Mr. Watkins came running up, holding the hoe.

"What's all the ruckus?" he asked.

"I think it's a fox," Billy said.

"It'll be a dead fox soon enough!" said Mr. Watkins as he threw open the door to the henhouse and went inside. A terrifying roar came out of the coop, and the boys screamed. Suddenly Mr. Watkins was thrown backward onto the dirt. His shirt was torn, and he was bleeding.

"Pa!" Tommy screamed.

Just then the rogue bear burst from the henhouse. Fang lunged at her, snapping at her legs.

The bear swatted at Fang, and the dog howled in pain. Tommy screamed again.

Johnny felt as if his feet were frozen in place. His heart was pounding so hard it seemed it would burst. The bear reeled up in front of him and roared.

Without thinking, Johnny grabbed Billy by the hand and ran. Billy was screaming loud enough to wake the dead.

"Run for the cabin!" Johnny shouted to Tommy. Billy slipped on the wet grass, and Johnny yanked him to his feet. He dragged Billy along like a rag doll.

The Watkinses' cabin door swung open suddenly, and Etta May staggered onto the porch. She hoisted her husband's long rifle to her shoulder and fired.

BOOM! The bear howled, turned, and ran.

Tommy ran to his mother. "Are you all right, Ma?"

"Where's your pa?" she asked.

Tommy's eyes filled with tears. Johnny swallowed hard. He didn't want to have to tell Mrs. Watkins that Big Tom was hurt—or maybe worse.

"He's fine," Johnny said, hoping it was true. "A little scratched up is all. Don't you worry about a thing."

"Look!" Billy cried, pointing.

Esau Stevens was running up the path. It had begun to rain, and drops drummed on his hat and dropped from his long face.

"Heard a heck of a commotion," he said, out of breath. "It's that bear, ain't it? Which way did she go?"

Billy pointed in the direction of the woods and then saw Davy and Georgie galloping up on their respective horses, Lightning and Soapy.

"We was out riding and heard a shot," Davy said, "and figured it was a little late for either huntin' or shootin' practice. What's going on?"

"The bear attacked Mr. Watkins!" Billy told Davy.

Etta May looked as if she were about to faint. Georgie caught her and carried her inside.

Davy ran to the henhouse and found Watkins still lying flat on his back. He was moaning and struggling to sit up.

"You've got a real nasty scratch there," Davy said, kneeling down next to him.

Watkins forced a smile. "I'll be fine," he said groggily. "Just help me to my feet."

"That bear knocked the wind clean out of you, Tom. It'd be best for you to rest a spell."

Watkins shook his head. "I gotta find Tommy and see to Etta May."

"They're all right," Davy said. "You will be, too."

"I'm much obliged, Davy," said Watkins. He blew out his breath, wincing at the pain. "Guess I will just sit me down a spell."

After a time Davy pulled Watkins's arm over his shoulder and gently helped him to his feet. They made their way slowly back to the cabin.

"What about the bear?" Watkins asked.

"Well," Davy said, "once I get you inside, I reckon Georgie and I'll go after that critter."

Inside the cabin, Georgie pulled another blanket over Etta May.

"She's awfully sick," he told Davy. "I can't believe

she found the strength to lift that rifle, much less fire it!"

Watkins, his chest wrapped in bandages, sat in a chair by the bed, brushing the damp hairs away from his wife's forehead.

"Mothers can do amazing things to defend their children," Davy told Georgie. "C'mon, let's get goin' while the trail is fresh."

Johnny and Billy were sitting at the Watkinses' kitchen table. "I'll go with you, Pa!" Johnny said, jumping up and walking to the door. "Just let me get my rifle!"

Davy held him back with a shake of his head. "This is serious business, Son," Davy said. "I'm afraid you just ain't got the experience to go hunting a persnickety she-bear."

"I hunted bear with you last winter," Johnny whined.

"That was different, Son. We were hunting turkeys and just happened upon a bear. This bear is more dangerous. She's in a proper frenzy." Davy put his hands reassuringly on Johnny's shoulders. "I need you to go home and take care of Billy, your ma, and little Maggie."

Davy told Watkins to have Tommy fetch Polly if his family needed anything. Outside the cabin Davy found Stevens waiting on the step.

"You goin' after that bear?" Stevens asked.

"Could be," Davy said.

"I'm coming, too!" Stevens said. Georgie winced.

Davy shrugged. "I reckon I can't stop you," he said. "But it's getting late, and we all better hurry before this trail washes away."

Davy quickly found tracks showing where the bear had turned and run.

Georgie bent down on one knee to examine the print. He dabbed at it with his finger. "Blood," said Georgie. "It looks like Etta May hit her."

Davy nodded. "But a shot that don't kill a bear only makes it madder."

At the edge of the woods they found a scarred tree trunk and bushes with broken branches.

Davy examined the long claw marks in the bark. "They're close together," he said. "They must have been made by a yearling cub climbing down."

Stevens frowned. "I killed that cub."

"A bear might have more than one a season," Davy said. "Reckon our she-bear sent her cub up this tree while she did her dangerous work."

Just then Stevens spun around. "I heard a bear growl!"

"Maybe," Davy said. He looked warily at Stevens. "Or it might just be thunder."

"Or maybe," Georgie said, "a little of both."

CHAPTER 5

The trail of an angry stampeding three-hundred-pound bear was not hard to follow.

With night coming, however, and the likelihood that the heavy rain might wash away familiar landmarks, the hunting party stopped at a sloped clearing to cut a blaze on a tree trunk to mark the way home. Then it continued its search for bear tracks.

"Here's a back foot," Georgie said, pointing to a faded six-inch-long print in the mud. There were five toes, with the big toe on the outside, and the marks of five sharp, straight claws.

"Here's a front one," Davy said. He put his arm out to stop Stevens from stumbling onto it. Davy smiled and pointed. "This here smaller track is headed in the opposite direction! This is one tricky bear," Davy added with admiration.

"Are you telling me," Stevens said sarcastically, "that

the great Davy Crockett doesn't know which way the bear went?"

"She went both ways," Davy said, "to confuse us."

Stevens chortled. "So this bear's smarter than both of you," he said mockingly.

Georgie took a step toward Stevens.

"Hold on there, now," Davy said, putting a hand on Georgie's shoulder. "No sense getting ornery just because the weather's bad. Let's take a look up in this direction. If the trail's no good, we'll double back."

Stevens agreed reluctantly.

After about half an hour of heavy slogging through mud and dense brush, Davy and Georgie stopped.

"What do you think?" Davy asked.

Georgie shrugged. "It's late and hard to see." He peered closely at a bush. "This bent twig *might* mean she passed this way. Then again, it might not."

"Maybe passed this way," snapped Stevens angrily, "maybe passed that way. We been tracking this bear half the night, and you two fools ain't got any better idea about where this bear is and where she isn't. I say we set a trap for her!"

Georgie rolled his eyes.

"I ain't normally one to argue," Davy said, "but in my experience—"

"Oh, the great woodsman speaks!" said Stevens in a mocking tone.

"Why, Davy's killed more bears in one season than you could count!" Georgie fumed.

"I'm surprised you can count at all!"

"That's it!" Georgie said, pushing up the sleeves of his shirt. "Let's settle this now, once and for all."

"Cool down now, fellers," Davy said. "We're here to kill a bear, not each other."

Georgie looked disappointed. Davy turned to Stevens. "Well, Mr. Stevens," he said, "I was only trying to make the point that you can't rightly know where to set a trap for a bear. They're unpredictable. And this particular critter has a powerful dislike of people. She'd likely smell you on your trap, no matter how ripe the bait. She's not an easy bear to trick."

Stevens listened, but from the sullen expression on his face it was obvious to Davy that he was not convinced.

"Anyway," said Davy, wiping his brow. "I sure wish this rain would let up." He turned to Georgie. "I calculate we're in her home turf. See what's left of that anthill?"

"Who cares about ants?" Stevens grumbled. "We're looking for a bear!"

"Don't you know anything?" Georgie snapped at Stevens. "Bears love to eat ants! They scoop up the hill and lick off the little critters that swarm onto their paw."

"Over in that bend is a bear tree," Davy said. "That's a sure sign."

The evergreen Davy was pointing to had bark clawed from the trunk and tooth marks in the soft wood. He knew that bears liked to eat the juicy tender layer just beneath a tree's bark. A clump of thick black hairs clung to the sticky sap where the bear had rubbed herself against the tree.

"Be quiet and follow me," Davy said. The three men inched along the trail while a gentle rain splattered on the leaves above their heads.

Not far from the bear tree, they found the half-buried remains of a deer.

"Oooh-wee, she's a mean critter," Georgie said. "Bears don't often kill anything bigger than a chipmunk."

"This deer probably got stuck in the rocks here," Davy said, moving closer to examine the carcass. He kicked away a soggy covering of leaves and twigs. "Front leg is broken. Hoof got stuck between these rocks."

Georgie nodded. "Guess that bear was hiding her meat till she could finish it."

Stevens groaned and held his nose. "Guess they like their meat pretty ripe."

Davy said, "Bears don't often kill their own game.

Usually they just eat whatever they happen to wander across, like this trapped deer."

Stevens wiped his nose on his sopping sleeve. "This is a waste of time," he said disgustedly. "You don't know what you're doing. We're going around in circles, and we're nowhere near that bear."

Stevens was surprised that neither Davy nor Georgie was paying him the slightest mind. He frowned. They were staring over his shoulder toward something in the woods. Finally Stevens had had enough. "What in thunderation is so interesting—" He turned to look over his shoulder, and his eyes nearly popped out of his skull.

Three hundred pounds of rogue she-bear was pounding toward them like a runaway train! Stevens's jaw dropped, and he went rigid with fright.

The bear skidded to a stop, reared up on her hind legs, and sniffed. Her eyes stared straight at Stevens as she rolled back her head and let out a terrifying roar. She dropped to all fours and lunged.

Stevens turned and ran. He looked back for just a second and saw Davy calmly hoist his rifle to his shoulder and shoot. BOOM! Without pausing to see if the bear was killed, Stevens turned around again and, quick as a rabbit, ran for home.

Davy's shot had only grazed the bear's thick skull.

"It's my turn," Georgie said.

But the bear was upon him before he could ready his rifle to shoot. The bear swatted away Georgie's rifle, and Georgie stumbled backward onto the ground. The bear reared up again and came down hard on Georgie's chest. Georgie felt like his ribs were about to cave in.

Suddenly the bear wheeled around. Davy was astraddle her back, stabbing at her furiously with his hunting knife.

Georgie rolled out from under the bear and quickly sucked in a huge gulp of air. The pain was unbearable. He took another deep, wheezing gulp and felt the sharp stab of several broken ribs.

Georgie dragged himself clear of the bear and heaved himself into a sitting position. He clutched gingerly at his chest. He looked up to see the bear whirling left and right. Davy was riding her like a wild horse. Georgie struggled to his feet.

"Hang in there, Davy!" he yelled. Georgie limped over to where his gun lay.

Suddenly the bear whipped around violently, and Davy was thrown clear. He landed on the ground with a painful *"Ooomph."*

For a split second the bear seemed confused. Davy had jumped to his feet and stood on one side of the bear; Georgie stood on the other. The bear swung her head heavily from side to side, sniffing, as if trying to decide in which direction to charge.

Suddenly Davy pointed and ran. "Get up that tree!" Davy hollered to Georgie as the bear charged.

Clutching at his ribs, Georgie managed to scramble up a pine tree, but the bear had succeeded in cutting Davy off.

Georgie gave a loud whistle. "Over here, Bruin-hilda!" he yelled, and rattled some branches.

Startled by the commotion, the bear turned and sniffed inquisitively. Georgie clung tightly, and the bear charged the pine tree. "Merciful thunder!" cried Georgie as the bear rocked the tree.

"Thank ye kindly!" Davy called to his friend as he shinnied up a tree. He swung his rifle across a low branch and grabbed the barrel, hauling himself up and out of reach of the bear.

"Don't mention it!" Georgie shouted, then fell silent as the bear shook the tree.

Georgie scrambled high into the smaller branches of the tree. The bear reached up with her front paws, then, with a sudden shove, pushed herself up the trunk. The tree swayed under her weight.

"Any ideas, friend?" Georgie called out anxiously to Davy.

"Break yourself a branch and slap her on the nose!" Davy said.

"Are you crazy?" Georgie screamed.

"Just do it!" Davy yelled. He was frustrated because he could not load his rifle while hanging from a branch.

"Ow! Consarnit!" Georgie cursed. The branch he had snapped cut into his palm.

"*RWOOOOORFF!*" roared the bear.

Georgie slapped the bear's nose. The bear howled and scooted tail first down the tree.

"It's the only tender part on 'em," Davy hollered.

"Well, now you get *your* chance!" Georgie said. "Why don't you just grin the old bear to death?"

"Reckon she's not in the mood for grinning," Davy said. "I haven't got enough teeth to charm this particular critter."

The bear now shinnied up Davy's tree. Davy quickly cut himself a branch with his hunting knife, and when the bear came within reach, he swatted her hard on the nose.

Davy knew that some bears were known for their smarts, some for their bad tempers. This one looked to be chock full of both.

The bear quickly scooted down the tree.

"Oh no," Georgie grumbled as the bear came sniffing at the base of his tree. He clutched at his ribs. "Do you think she's ever going to get tired of this? I sure am!"

Georgie whacked the bear's nose, and she let out a surprised howl. Her face was so close that Georgie could feel the blast of her breath. The bear crawled down from the tree and found Georgie's discarded rifle on the ground.

"My best rifle!" Georgie whined as the bear crunched it between her jaws. "I loved that gun."

"So does she," Davy teased. "Maybe that'll satisfy her and she'll go away."

But the gun wasn't enough for the bear. She paced around the trees. She climbed up one, then the other, driven back by slaps on her nose until sunset.

"Are we stuck here all night?" Georgie asked. "I'm hungry and wet. We might as well be in Florida with the army!"

Davy laughed. "She's bound to leave soon to tend to her cub," he said.

Sure enough, the bear finally seemed to lose interest and ambled off. Davy and Georgie waited, then cautiously climbed down from their trees. "Well," Davy said, "thank the stars that's over."

No sooner had Davy set moccasin to soil than the bear came charging back.

Davy had been treed by bears before, but he reckoned he set a new record this time. He was up that tree so fast, his feet were in the branches before his head.

It was dark now and getting cold. "At least the rain's stopped," said Georgie, trying to be agreeable. He shifted uncomfortably and winced.

"How are you doing?" Davy called out. He knew Georgie was in awful pain.

"Well, I was too scared to hurt before," Georgie said. He tried to chuckle. "Now I'm too tired to be scared."

"I reckon you ought to take your possibles bag and use the strap to tie yourself to the tree," Davy suggested. "I calculate Mrs. Bear is going to be spending the night in our company."

Georgie shivered in his damp buckskins. A lonely

owl hooted, then Davy and Georgie heard the mournful cry of the whippoorwills.

Georgie looked down and wearily shook his head. The bear paced back and forth under the tree like a faithful sentry.

"Maybe I should sing her a lullaby," he suggested. He began to sing, and after a time the bear settled down sleepily at the base of Georgie's tree.

Georgie sang until he was hoarse.

Later that night the clouds cleared away, and a quarter moon rose in the sky. Davy chewed on some parched corn from his possibles bag.

"I'm plumb sung out," Georgie croaked exhaustedly. "You think that critter's going to get tired and leave? She's even more messed up than I am."

"Bears can take a lot of punishment," said Davy. "I heard tell of one who took ten rifle balls and an ax in the head and came roaring back for more." He took another bite of corn. "Sometimes bullets don't pierce their protective layer of fat. This one must've eaten awfully well before winter. She's mighty hefty for a spring bear."

"I'll say!" said Georgie.

" 'Course, eating is what bears do best," Davy said, and paused. He put away his possibles pouch and crossed his arms behind his head. "Did I ever tell you about the time I came back to my cabin and found a bear sitting at the table eating molasses out of my jug?"

"No," said Georgie, "I don't recollect you ever did."

"Why, I hollered and screamed and sent that critter running three-legged, holding up a pawful of molasses," said Davy. "When he got to the river, that old bear held that sticky paw over the water. Weren't a minute before that paw was crawling with flies, and the next thing you know a big fat trout jumped up for the bait."

Davy grinned to himself. "That bear swatted the trout onto the shore and then caught another! Pretty soon that bear had a huge heap of fish piled up on the bank, pretty as you please. Then he sat down and ate 'em. I got hungry just looking." Davy laughed and shook his head.

"When he got up to leave, the bear looked back and waved at me. Then he ambled off into the woods. Well, you know what I found on the shore?"

"No," Georgie said. "What did you find?"

"Four fat trout laid out in a row—not a bad trade for part of a jug of molasses. That just goes to show you," Davy said philosophically, "bears are like folks. Some are sociable, and some are ornery."

Georgie yawned. "Well, all I can say is I wish this bear would learn some manners."

Davy yawned, too. " 'Fraid it's too late for that."

The next morning Davy was startled awake by the sound of a dog barking. His first thought was that he was back home and the dogs were barking for breakfast. But the rough tree bark against his cheek and the crick in his neck were painful reminders of where he really was.

Davy looked down. It was Whirlwind! Davy let out a whoop. "Attaboy, Whirlwind!"

The dog was nipping at the bear's tail. When the bear turned, Whirlwind ran. The dog made a tight circle so that in trying to grab him, the bear ran around and around as if she were chasing her own stumpy tail.

After a few minutes the bear, dizzy and dazed, sat down with a thump.

Whirlwind barked and ran off into the woods. The angry bear lumbered to her feet and stumbled after him.

"C'mon!" Davy called out to Georgie as he scrambled down from his tree.

Georgie groaned. His broken ribs stabbed at him like knives as he half climbed and half fell down the tree.

Davy helped Georgie to his feet and hastily loaded his rifle. "Let's get you out of here before Mrs. Bear gets tired of chasing Whirlwind's tail."

Georgie tried to stand, then buckled from the pain. "Davy, you gotta get that bear," Georgie muttered. "I've got me a powerful grudge."

"You can have her paws for breakfast!" Davy said. He looked to where the bear had run off. "I can't say I'm feeling too fond of that critter myself."

CHAPTER 7

"Whirlwind's the best dog I ever owned," Davy declared.

"Amen to that," Georgie mumbled weakly.

"Soon as I catch that bear," Davy resolved, "I'm gonna give Whirlwind that critter's liver to eat with some fresh biscuits!"

"Biscuits," Georgie moaned. "I sure could . . ."

Georgie collapsed. Davy caught him and hoisted him onto his shoulders. It would be a long walk at best, Davy thought. Having to carry Georgie would only add to the miles. "Well," Davy said to himself, "maybe that she-bear is even more tired than I am."

The blazed trunks were easy to find and follow. The trip back took a long time because Davy had to stop often to rest.

Davy was mighty glad to see the smoke from the

Watkins cabin's chimney about the time the sun was at its highest.

Tom Watkins was sitting on his porch whittling a new hoe handle. Clean white bandages were wrapped around his chest.

Little Tommy ran up to greet Davy.

"What happened, Mr. Crockett? Did you kill that bear?" Tommy asked.

"Not yet," Davy said. "But we did tire her out some."

Holding his side, Big Tom walked up to Davy. "Is Georgie all right?"

" 'Fraid he's a bit sore after dancing with Mrs. Bear," Davy said.

Watkins nodded. "Well, she does trod a man's toes. I thought Esau was out hunting with you," he said as he helped Davy lower Georgie gently to the ground.

"He was," Davy said, "but we haven't seen him since yesterday afternoon. He seemed a mite shy once he met Mrs. Bear face to snout. He ran off so fast he clean left his own shadow behind."

Watkins sighed. "Esau's not really a bad feller. Just doesn't know nearly as much as he thinks he does."

Watkins helped Davy give Georgie a dipper of fresh well water.

Georgie's eyes flickered open. "Where are we?" he asked. "And where's that bear?"

Davy grinned. "Glad to see you, Mr. Russel. We're visiting a spell at the Watkins farm, but we'll be heading back to the Crockett cabin directly. Are you up to it?"

Georgie reached for the ladle and took a deep swallow of water. "Reckon I can make it if you can."

"I'd appreciate it if I could borrow your wagon," Davy said.

"You're welcome to it," Watkins told Davy. Together they eased Georgie onto the wagon bed.

"How's Etta May?" Davy asked, settling onto the creaky seat.

"She's feeling much better," Watkins said.

"Maybe shooting bears agrees with her," Davy said. "Gee-up!" Davy flicked the reins, and the old plow horse snorted and began a slow plod down the hill.

Whirlwind was the first to greet Davy and Georgie upon their return.

"I'll never call that dog worthless again!" Georgie declared.

Johnny and Billy ran up with Bullet and Blue. "What happened, Pa? Ma's been worrying her hair white!" Johnny hollered.

"I knew this would happen," Polly said, racing up to the wagon. She clucked her tongue at the sight of Georgie.

"Now don't go on," Davy said.

"I'll be fine just as soon as I have some of your home cooking," Georgie said, but his voice was raspy and weak.

With much bustling and barking and general commotion, the Crocketts got Georgie into the cabin and settled him on a pallet before the fire. Polly fretted and fussed over Georgie as she bound his broken ribs and cleaned his scrapes.

"I reckon he'll sleep for quite a spell," Davy concluded.

Later, Davy sat with Polly in front of the fire.

"Old Whirlwind drew that bear off like Christmas wrapping off a present. I reckon he led her a merry chase!" Davy smiled and reached down to give the dog a pat on the head. "That bear might never come back!"

Whirlwind's tail thumped happily on the packed dirt floor.

"Reckon if I'd took a bath like you're always squawking about," Davy teased, "Whirlwind would never have found us through all that rain."

"Well, you better take one now," Polly said, getting up from her chair. She waved her hand under her nose. "By thunder, but you smell like a bear yourself."

Johnny and Billy laughed. Then Polly sent them to fetch the bathwater.

Polly sighed. "I'm glad this rogue hunting is all over," she said.

Davy stared into the coals of the fire and shrugged.

"Maybe it is, and maybe it isn't," he said.

Polly looked stunned. "Truth is," Davy said, "she might be coming back. The Indians know that the only thing to do when a bear goes rogue is hunt it down." He turned in his chair to look at her. "You never can tell what it's going to do."

"Well, I don't want you hunting that bear," Polly said angrily. "What if that was you, busted all up, instead of poor Georgie?"

Davy shrugged. "That's a chance I'll have to take." He turned back to the fire. "But this time I'll get up a hunting party like the Indians do. Esau turned tail and Georgie's out, but I'm sure I can get some other fellers to join me. 'Course, I'd have to split the reward."

"There's no amount of money worth what Georgie's been through," Polly said.

Georgie had awakened and was sitting up in bed. "Amen to that," he said.

"Polly, we need that money," Davy said.

Polly twisted her hands nervously in the folds of her skirt. "We can get by without the money," she said. "You said so yourself. We can cut down and make do."

"Polly," Davy said gently, "you know as well as I

do that we're already cut so close to the bone there ain't nothin' left to scrape."

"What am I supposed to do if you get hurt?" Polly demanded angrily. "I can't go out and hunt, and it will be years before Johnny is old enough to take care of anyone else."

"Ain't nothin' going to happen to me," Davy tried to assure her.

Polly sat down heavily in a chair and sighed. "This whole last year with you away I nearly worried myself to death, Davy. I never knew when—or if—you was coming home."

Davy got up from his chair and took Polly's hands in his. "Polly, you mean more to me than anything in the world," he told her. "But this is something I just have to do."

Polly nodded and said, "I know."

Johnny stood outside the cabin door with a water bucket sloshing by his knees. Billy was standing behind him. He held his bucket in two hands and half carried, half dragged it across the porch.

"Go on in!" Billy said.

"Hush," Johnny said. "Ma and Pa is tangling about something." He felt strange listening to his parents argue. It didn't happen often, but when it did it almost always had something to do with money—or in the case of the Crocketts, the lack of money.

"C'mon, Johnny," Billy complained, "I'm getting soaked." Billy had somehow managed to spill almost all the water from the bucket onto his pants.

"You just hush up, Billy. I got some serious thinking to do." Johnny sat down on the edge of his bucket. Billy decided he might as well sit down, too.

"What are we thinking about?" Billy asked after a time.

"I need me a plan to make some money," Johnny said.

"What for?" Billy asked.

"So's Ma and Pa won't have to worry about money no more and never have to argue again."

Billy nodded. Imitating his brother, he leaned forward with his chin in the cup of his hands. After a quiet minute Billy turned to Johnny. "It ain't working," he said.

"I've got it!" Johnny said.

"What?" Billy asked.

Johnny smiled and jumped up. He took hold of his bucket. "I've got the perfect plan!" he said.

Polly woke while the sky was still dark. Davy snored gently beside her, with little Maggie curled up on his chest contentedly sucking her thumb.

Fear stirred in Polly's heart. She could tell that something was wrong. By the light of the fire's embers she could see Georgie on his pallet. Whirlwind, Bullet, and Blue were curled up at his feet.

Polly crept from beneath the quilts and padded over to the ladder leading to the boys' sleeping loft. She climbed up the rough wooden rungs and peeked into the loft.

Billy was all rolled up in his quilt—but Johnny was gone!

"Davy!" Polly cried.

Davy sat up so fast, little Maggie tumbled into his lap and started to cry. The dogs leapt to their feet, running and barking in all directions.

"What in tarnation?" Davy blurted.

"Johnny's gone!" cried Polly.

Davy gently put Maggie down on the bed. "Now Polly," he said, "the boy may just be answering the call of nature." Then he looked at the gun rack.

"Thunderation," Davy said, and began pulling on his buckskins.

"Where would he go?" Polly asked frantically.

Davy knew, but he didn't want to say.

"He went after that bear, didn't he?" Polly demanded.

"Reckon so," Davy said. "But don't worry. He

can't have gotten far. I'll find him and be back directly."

Johnny followed the blazes his father had cut and soon found himself deep in the woods beyond the Watkins farm. He found Georgie's chewed-up rifle beneath two well-clawed trees.

"You and me'll get that old bear," Johnny told his rifle. "And Ma and Pa will get the reward money. And won't they be proud of me!"

Johnny could see where the bear had run off after Whirlwind, but he didn't know if he should follow that trail or look for fresher signs. Johnny decided finally to follow the old trail until fresher signs appeared.

The old trail looped around and around. Johnny smiled faintly to himself, picturing Whirlwind capering from tree to tree, teasing that big bear. After a time the trail seemed to break up, and Johnny realized that he was alone deep in the woods, unsure what to do next.

Johnny leaned wearily against a tree. His arms ached from carrying the heavy Kentucky rifle. Maybe I better just go home, he thought sadly. He stood up straight and felt something tug at his shirt. He turned and saw black hairs stuck in a trickle of amber sap. "This is a bear's scratching tree!" Johnny exclaimed. He had learned this from his father.

By the thin light of dawn Johnny searched the ground for fresh tracks. Sure enough, there in the mud he saw bear prints. Johnny winked at his rifle and whispered, "Looks like you and me are gonna bag that old bear after all!"

Johnny found many tracks, old and new, covering a thicket. He figured this was a spot the bear came to often.

Then he saw a huge fallen oak. Its gnarled roots hung like a ragged curtain over the base of its upturned trunk.

Behind the roots slept the she-bear and her cub.

Johnny's hands trembled. "Stay calm and be sure of your mark." Johnny remembered his father's words, so he decided to creep around and find an angle that would give him a clear shot. He could not afford to have his bullet deflected by the thick roots.

As he moved, Johnny kept his eyes locked on the sleeping bears. He shuffled sideways slowly and quietly, one moccasin at a time. His foot bumped into a large hollow log, and as he lifted his leg over the log and put his foot down, he felt something tighten around his ankle. Suddenly the world was upside down, and Johnny was swinging in the air! His body slammed against the hard tree trunk.

KABOOM! Johnny's gun went off, and he heard the bullet ricochet.

"You little fool!" a voice cried out. "You spoiled my trap!"

Johnny hung upside down by his tethered ankle, swinging back and forth against the tree trunk. He watched the bear scramble out of her den and swat her cub, who yelped and scrambled up a tree to safety. Then the mother bear stood up on her hind legs and gave a mighty roar!

Johnny didn't have time to say a prayer or even wonder what would happen next. He felt a tug on his ankle and heard a snapping sound. He fell facedown onto the ground. He rolled to his knees just in time to see Esau Stevens lift his fancy rifle to his shoulder. Johnny followed Stevens's wide-eyed stare to the mother black bear poised to charge.

"Get out of here!" Stevens screeched to Johnny.

Johnny scrambled inside a nearby hollow log just as Stevens fired. *KABOOM!* Gray gun smoke tinted the air and gave off a bitter tang. The bullet sang harmlessly through the leaves—and the bear was on Stevens in a flurry of claws.

CHAPTER 8

KABOOM!

Johnny poked his head out of the log at the sound of a second shot. He watched the bear charge again and saw his father quickly reload his rifle.

"Pa!" Johnny yelled.

Bullet, Whirlwind, and Blue ran past Johnny to harass the bear. The big beast swatted at the dogs, who jumped just beyond her reach.

The three-hundred-pound bear turned and grabbed Davy in a death hug. The dogs barked and howled and snapped at the bear's legs, but she would not let go of her prey.

Davy wrestled the bear, stabbing at her with his hunting knife over and over. He could feel the hot blast of her breath as her huge jaws swung inches from his face. Desperate, Davy bit down hard on the bear's nose. Startled, the bear loosened her grip.

Davy staggered backward and tried to catch his breath, but again the bear lunged. Davy grabbed hold of his knife with both hands, and when the bear came down on him, he thrust upward with every ounce of strength he had.

The bear stumbled, took a few awkward steps, staggered, and finally collapsed with great chuffing breaths. The dogs grew silent and cautiously circled the still bear.

Davy felt like his insides had been squeezed out of him. Even so, he swept up Johnny in his arms and gave him a hug.

"I'm mighty glad to see you, Johnny, but I'm gonna tan your hide," he said.

Johnny was too happy to complain.

Davy put his son down and strode to where Stevens lay. He didn't appear to be hurt too badly, and Davy helped him to his feet.

"Mighty glad you came by, Mr. Crockett, or that bear would've had me for breakfast," Stevens said.

"Always glad to help a neighbor in need," Davy replied. He used the shreds of Stevens's shirt to bandage his wounds.

"Saw what you did there," Stevens said. "That was mighty brave." Then, as if the words hurt more than the bear scratches, he said softly, "I guess you really *are* the best hunter in these woods."

Stevens extended his hand for Davy to shake.

"Reckon you earned that bounty, Mr. Crockett," he said with a smile.

Davy shook his head. "I reckon there's enough for both of us. And enough meat, too."

Then they heard a sorrowful cry. The cub had scuttled down the tree and was nuzzling his mother, prodding her gently with his head.

"Poor little feller," Davy said. "What's he gonna do without a mama?"

CHAPTER 9

avid Crockett!" scolded Polly. "What do you think you're doing bringing a bear cub into this house?"

"It's just for a little while, Polly. Till we help him get a new ma," Davy explained. "He'd likely die on his own."

"I don't see how that's our problem," Polly said. But she knew there was no changing Davy's mind. Once he thought he was right, he'd just go ahead anyway.

"The cub needs a name," Billy said.

Johnny patted the bear cub's head. "What're we gonna call him, Pa?"

Davy stroked his chin.

"What about Death Hug?" Georgie called from his pallet by the fire. "After his ma's affectionate ways."

"I like it!" Davy said. "Death Hug it is."

The little bear rolled onto his back, and Johnny

scratched the cub's stomach. Death Hug gratefully licked Johnny's face.

"Why don't you take him outside and give him the last of those nuts we used to lure him home?" Davy suggested.

Johnny led the cub outside. "C'mon, Death Hug! Let's you and me wrassle!"

"Me first!" Billy cried.

Davy stood in the open doorway, watching his son and the small bear tumble over and over on the soft grass.

For the next few weeks Georgie mended, and the boys and the dogs romped with little Death Hug. The cub was so cute and cuddly that Davy kept finding one reason and another to put off taking him back to the woods. The boys were having such a good time that Davy hated to end their fun.

The cub was so clever he could fetch just as well as the dogs. He climbed trees as easily as a monkey and would stand on his hind legs and dance for a lick of molasses.

Of course, Death Hug also dug up Polly's new flower bed, looking for tasty roots and ants; pulled laundry off the line; and chewed through a table leg as if it were a toothpick.

One morning when Davy and Georgie were giving

Johnny a shooting lesson, Polly came out to call them in to breakfast. When they walked into the cabin, Death Hug was standing on a chair licking out Billy's bowl of corn mush.

"Get down from there, you varmint!" Polly snapped.

Startled, Death Hug knocked over the chair. The mush bowl spun around and fell to the floor with a crash, and Death Hug ran to hide under the bed.

"Look at this!" said Polly. "Broke a bowl and busted this chair. Don't you think it's time you found him a new ma?"

"Reckon you're right," Davy agreed.

"Do we have to, Pa?" whined Johnny.

"He's a wild critter and belongs in the woods," Davy said. "First thing tomorrow we'll start looking."

Early the next morning Davy and Johnny set out for the woods. Death Hug shuffled along behind.

Davy tried to explain. "Now, you see, Son, we can't teach him all the things a proper bear needs to know about foraging and hunting and finding all kinds of food year-round. Death Hug needs to know how to find his own way in the woods, mark a proper bear trail, and build a winter den."

Davy stopped on the trail and put his arm around Johnny's shoulders. Death Hug rolled onto his back and kicked playfully at the air. Davy and Johnny laughed at his antics.

"The thing is, Johnny," Davy said, "to be safe on his own, Death Hug needs to fear humans and other bears, too. Only a mama bear can teach him all that. And mama bears are quite strict. If a cub doesn't pay attention, he gets a swat on the bottom." They resumed their walk along the trail.

"Now, Mrs. Bear isn't doing that to be mean," Davy explained. "She's making sure that the memory sticks."

"Bears sure are a lot like people," Johnny observed ruefully, recalling the licking he'd gotten after he'd gone off hunting alone.

"The Indians know that," Davy agreed. "They respect the bear. Their medicine men wear bear hides during their most sacred ceremonies. The Indian knows the bear is a powerful, smart critter."

"Death Hug's real smart," Johnny said. "Couldn't we teach him to live with us?" He glanced back at the cub lumbering along behind them, faithful as a dog.

Davy shook his head. "He's right cute now, Johnny. But a male black bear can weigh up to six hundred pounds! You don't think your ma would let him sleep by the fire, do you? There wouldn't hardly be any room for us."

"We could build a shed," Johnny suggested.

Davy put his hand on Johnny's shoulder and said simply, "Bears need room."

"But Death Hug and his mama shared a pretty small den," Johnny tried to argue.

"It's nature's way that he live free," Davy said firmly. "We have no right to mess with that."

Johnny sighed. "I guess you're right."

"Now lookee here," Davy said, pointing to a battered berry bush. "See the way these bushes have been chewed. That's a bear sign. They don't just eat blackberries—they gobble the bushes, twigs and all. This is fresh. We'll just have to see if it's a mama or papa bear."

Toward the end of a long day of searching, Davy spotted a she-bear digging roots with her yearling cub. He and Johnny found a safe place to hide, and watched. Death Hug gave a loud bellow. The she-bear looked up from her meal and sniffed the air. She moaned, then slapped the ground. Her cub shinnied up the nearest tree.

Death Hug waddled hesitantly toward the she-bear and brayed. The she-bear ran to meet him. She stopped suddenly and sniffed.

"She doesn't like that man smell," Davy whispered to Johnny.

The she-bear sniffed again. Death Hug whimpered. Then the she-bear licked the cub's face.

After a few moments the she-bear allowed her cub to

climb down from the tree. Soon he and Death Hug were wrestling and playing like brothers.

"Reckon we can leave now," Davy whispered.

Back at the cabin Polly said, "Well, Mr. Crockett. Are you fixing to join any wars or bear hunts soon, or are you planning to stay a while?"

"I calculate I better stick around, at least till I teach these boys to be men," Davy said.

"Shucks, Pa, can't we be bears instead?" Johnny teased. Davy smiled and gave him a big bear hug.

EPILOG

Davy Crockett is perhaps the most famous folk hero of the American frontier. He was born in 1786 and grew up in the rugged country of eastern Tennessee, where his father ran a small country inn. Business was never very good, and the family often relied on young Davy's hunting skills to put food on the table. But even in tough times, Davy had a knack for amusing himself and others with tall tales, a skill that was to later become part of the Crockett legend.

In 1806, Davy married Polly Finley, and they began to raise a family. As the frontier grew more crowded with settlers, Davy and Polly kept moving their family farther west. In 1813, Davy and his family settled on a small farm in western Tennessee.

Davy championed the rights of Native Americans in an era marked by great injustice toward Indian people. In 1813, he joined the army in an effort to negotiate an end to the Creek War. His efforts were successful, and in the process he earned the respect of both sides.

Davy returned from the war a hero and was so popular that he was eventually elected to the United States Congress, where he served three terms. During that time, he helped draft a treaty that would have enabled the Indian people to keep their land. But in 1835, when Congress decided to break the treaty, and his efforts to save it failed, he decided not to run for reelection.

In 1836, Davy Crockett, along with his trusted companion Georgie Russel, joined a small band of brave American settlers under siege at the Alamo in San Antonio, Texas, which was then part of Mexico. The settlers fought long and valiantly in the name of freedom to defend themselves against the Mexican Army, but in the end their numbers were no match for the huge force amassed against them. The enemy soldiers finally overran the Alamo, killing every man, woman, and child within its walls. Davy Crockett died as he had lived—an American hero. And the phrase "Remember the Alamo!" lived on to inspire and unite the Americans in Texas, who eventually won their freedom from Mexico and brought Texas into the United States.